CONTENTS

4 How to use this book
6 What to take
8 About flowers
9 Shapes to look for
10 Flowers, fruits and seeds
12 Leaves
14 Yellow flowers
22 Blue flowers
26 Pink flowers
34 Purple flowers
38 Red flowers
40 White and green flowers
55 Protecting wild flowers
56 Flower notebook
57 Photographing flowers
58 Useful words
59 Internet links
60 Scorecard
63 Index

HOW TO USE THIS BOOK

This book is an identification guide to some of the wild flowers of Britain and Europe. Take it with you when you go out spotting.

The flowers are arranged by colour to make it easy for you to look them up. This Rosebay Willowherb, for example, appears in the section of the book that shows pink flowers. The picture in the circle below shows a close-up of a Rosebay Willowherb seed, to help you identify the plant. Sometimes there are close-ups of flowers or fruits, too.

Top of plant

Rosebay Willowherb

The height of a plant is measured from its top to ground level

Seed of Rosebay Willowherb (seeds can be seen after the plant has finished flowering)

Ground level

Usborne Spotter's Guides
WILD FLOWERS

Christopher J. Humphries
Department of Botany, The Natural History Museum

Illustrated by Hilary Burn

Wild flowers consultant: Richard Scott
Edited by Rosie Dickins, Jessica Datta and Sue Jacquemier
Series editor: Philippa Wingate
Designed by Nicola Butler
Cover designer: Michael Hill
Series designer: Laura Fearn
Additional illustrations by Victoria Goaman, Ian Jackson and Michelle Ross

Acknowledgements:
Cover: © Positive image/Alamy; 1 © David Boag/Alamy;
2-3, 6-7 © Tony Stone Images; 8-9 © Landlife; 56-57 © CORBIS.
Backgrounds: 4-5, 10-55, 58-62 © Digital Vision;

This edition first published in 2006 by Usborne Publishing Ltd.,
Usborne House, 83-85 Saffron Hill, London
EC1N 8RT, England. www.usborne.com

Printed in China

HOW FLOWERS ARE DESCRIBED

Each flower in this book has a picture and a description to help you to identify it. The example below shows you how the descriptions work.

Picture of flower (not drawn to scale)

Name and description of flower

➡ SCARLET PIMPERNEL
Grows along the ground. Flowers close in bad weather. Black dots under the pointed, oval leaves. Cultivated land. Where to find flower
15cm tall. June-Aug.

Average height of plant

When to see plant in flower

Flowers may also be blue

Close-up of flower with additional information to help identify plant

Circle to tick when you spot this flower

AREAS COVERED BY THIS BOOK

The green area on this map shows the countries which are covered by this book. Not all the flowers that grow in these areas appear in the book, and some flowers are more common in one country than another.

Scandinavia

British Isles

Mainland Europe

Throughout this book, you will find suggested links to wild flowers websites. For a complete list of links and instructions, turn to page 59.

WHAT TO TAKE

When you go out to spot flowers, take the following items with you:

- this book;

- a notepad and a pencil, so that you can record your finds;

- a tape measure, to measure plants;

- a magnifying glass, so you can examine individual flowers and any insects you may find;

- a camera (if you have one), to photograph flowers (see page 57).

Draw the flowers you spot, and note down when and where you found them. Write down the height of the plant, and the colour and shape of the flower heads and leaves. If you see a flower that is not in this book, your notes will help you to identify it from other books later. Don't pick wild flowers – see page 55 for more about protecting them.

For links to two online guides to identifying wild flowers, turn to page 59.

SCORECARD

The scorecard at the end of this book gives you a score for each flower you spot. A common flower scores 5 points, and a very rare one is worth 25 points. If you like, you can add up your score after a day out spotting. Some flowers may not be common where you live. Try to spot them if you go on holiday. Other flowers are rare in the wild.

Species (Name of flower)	Score	Date spotted
Daisy	5	20/07/06
Dandelion	5	
Deptford Pink	25	26/08/06
Devil's Bit Scabious	10	17/07/06

Fill in the scorecard like this.

Count rare flowers if you see them in a garden or on television.

7

ABOUT FLOWERS

These pictures show some different kinds of flowers, and explain some of the words that appear in the book. When you are examining a plant, look closely at the flowerhead to help you to identify it.

Some flowers have petals of even length and lots of stamens.

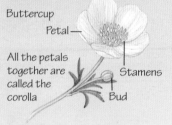

Buttercup

Petal

All the petals together are called the corolla

Stamens

Bud

The petals of some flowers are joined together.

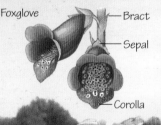

Foxglove

Bract

Sepal

Corolla

Some flowerheads are made up of clusters of tiny flowers.

Daisy

Centre is really lots of tiny flowers

Some flowers have petals which form hoods and lips.

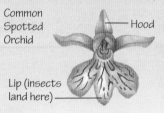

Common Spotted Orchid

Hood

Lip (insects land here)

Toadflax

The petals of some flowers form a tube called a spur.

Spur (contains nectar which is drunk by bees)

SHAPES TO LOOK FOR

These pictures show some of the different ways that plants grow. If you look out for these shapes, it will help you to recognize different plants.

An "erect" plant grows straight up from the ground. "Runners" are stems that grow sideways along the ground, as though they are creeping. Some plants grow in thick mats or carpets close to the ground. These are called "mat-forming" plants.

An erect plant

Early Purple Orchid

A mat-forming plant

Stonecrop

A plant with runners

Runner

Creeping Buttercup

FLOWERS, FRUITS AND SEEDS

This is what the inside of a Buttercup looks like. The stigma, style and ovary together form the female part of the flower, or "carpel". The stamens are the male parts. Pollen from the stamens is received by the stigma (this is called pollination). It causes seeds to grow inside the ovary.

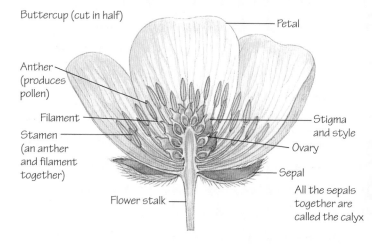

Buttercup (cut in half)

Petal

Anther (produces pollen)

Filament

Stamen (an anther and filament together)

Stigma and style

Ovary

Sepal

All the sepals together are called the calyx

Flower stalk

Some flowers can pollinate themselves and some are pollinated by wind. Other flowers need insects to spread their pollen. These flowers have special scents and markings to attract insects.

The scent and colour of this Meadow Clary flower have attracted a bee

Pollen brushes onto the bee; when it visits another flower, the stigma will pick up this pollen from its body

10

FROM FLOWER TO FRUIT

A flower helps a plant to produce seeds. Once a flower is pollinated, the seeds start to develop and the petals wither and fall off. The rest of the flower becomes a fruit containing seeds.

A bee pollinates the Poppy flower

The petals and stamens die

The ovary swells and develops into a fruit

FRUITS AND SEEDS

The seeds of a plant are usually surrounded by a fruit. Different plants have different-looking fruits, so you can recognize plants by their fruits. Here are two examples.

Remains of flower

Seed

Blackberry fruit
(the seeds are inside)

Rosehip
(fruit of Dog
Rose) cut in half

Remains of flower

11

For a link to a website introducing plant biology, turn to page 59.

LEAVES

Even if a plant is not in flower, you can recognize it from its leaves. There are many different leaf shapes.

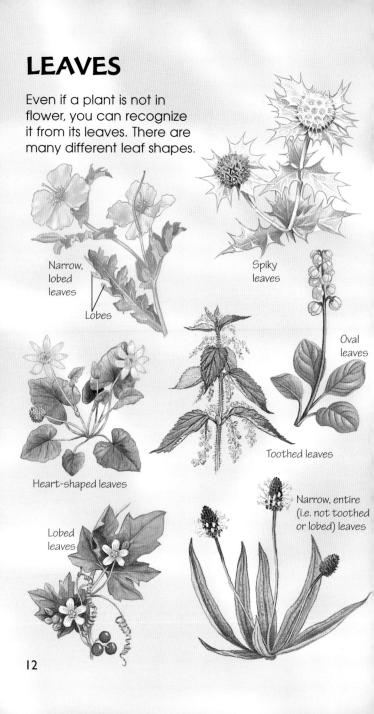

Narrow, lobed leaves

Lobes

Spiky leaves

Oval leaves

Heart-shaped leaves

Toothed leaves

Lobed leaves

Narrow, entire (i.e. not toothed or lobed) leaves

Leaves can also be arranged in different ways on the stem of a plant.

Leaves growing in whorls around the stem

Leaves growing in a rosette around the base of the stem

Leaves growing alternately on the stem

Leaves growing in opposite pairs on the stem

Leaves growing in a spiral around the stem

YELLOW FLOWERS

Look for these flowers in damp places, such as ditches, marshes and water meadows.

➡ LESSER CELANDINE
A small, creeping plant with glossy, heart-shaped leaves. Shiny yellow flowers. Look in damp, shady woods and waysides. 7cm tall. March-May.

◀ ALTERNATE-LEAVED GOLDEN SAXIFRAGE
Small plant with round, toothed leaves and greenish-yellow flowers. Look in wet places. 7cm tall. April-July.

Each flower has four yellow sepals

➡ CREEPING BUTTERCUP
Look for the long runners near the ground. Hairy, deeply divided leaves. Shiny yellow flowers. Common weed of grassy places. May-Aug.

Runner

➡ CREEPING JENNY

A creeping, mat-forming plant with shiny, oval leaves. Yellow flowers are 1.5-2.5cm across. In grassy places and under hedges. June-Aug.

Opposite leaves

➡ COWSLIP

Easily recognized in April and May by the single clusters of nodding flowers. Rosette of leaves at base. Grows in meadows. 15cm tall.

Sepals

Close-up of flower

⬅ COMMON MEADOW RUE

Tall, erect plant with dense clusters of flowers. Leaves have 3-4 lobes. Look in marshy fields and fens. Up to 80cm tall. July-Aug.

15

YELLOW FLOWERS

Look for these flowers in woods, hedgerows and heaths.

Cluster of fruits

➡ HERB BENNET or WOOD AVENS
Fruits have hooks which catch on clothes and animals' fur. Woods, hedges and shady places. Up to 50cm tall. June-Aug.

⬅ YELLOW PIMPERNEL
Like Creeping Jenny, but smaller, with more pointed leaves. Slender, trailing stems. The flowers close in dull weather. Woods and hedges. May-Sept.

Barberries can be used to make jam

➡ BARBERRY
A shrub with spiny branches. Bees visit the drooping flowers. Look for the red berries. Hedges and scrubland. Up to 100cm tall. May-June.

← WOOD GROUNDSEL

Erect plant growing on heaths and sandy soil. The petals of the small flowers curl back. Narrow lobed leaves. 60cm tall. July-Sept.

Close-up of flower

→ YELLOW ARCHANGEL

Also called Weasel-Snout. Look for the red-brown markings on the yellow petals. Opposite pairs of leaves. Common in woods. 40cm tall. May-June.

Whorl of flowers

← PRIMROSE

Well-known spring flower, with hairy stems and rosette of large leaves. Often grows in patches. Woods, hedges and fields. 15cm tall. Dec.-May.

YELLOW FLOWERS

Look for these flowers in open, grassy places, such as heaths and commons.

🔖 FURZE

Also called Gorse or Whin. Dark green, spiny bush on heaths and commons. The bright yellow flowers smell like almonds. 100-200cm tall. March-June.

Close-up of flower

➡ BIRD'S FOOT TREFOIL

Also called Bacon and Eggs because the yellow flowers are streaked with red. Look for this small, creeping plant on grassy banks and downs. May-June.

The seed pods look like birds' claws

Seeds

Silverweed

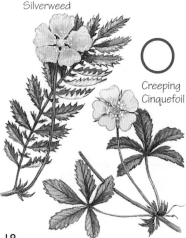

Creeping Cinquefoil

⬅ CREEPING CINQUEFOIL

Like Silverweed, spreads close to the ground with long, rooting runners. Hedge banks and grassy places. May-Aug.

◀ COMMON ST. JOHN'S WORT
Look for see-through dots on the narrow, oval leaves, and black dots on the petals and sepals. Damp, grassy places. 60cm tall. June-Sept.

➡ WOAD
Look for the hanging pods on this tall, erect plant. The leaves were once boiled to make a blue dye. Waysides and dry places. 70cm tall. June-Sept.

Seed pod

Dandelion "clock"

◀ DANDELION
Common weed with rosette of toothed leaves. The flowers close at night. Look for the "clock" of downy white fruits. Waysides. 15cm tall. March-June.

Close-up of fruit

19

For a link to a website about wild flowers found in Britain, turn to page 59.

YELLOW FLOWERS

➡ STONECROP
Also called Wallpepper.
Mat-forming plant with
star-shaped flowers.
The thick, fleshy leaves
have a peppery taste.
Dunes, shingle and
walls. June-July.

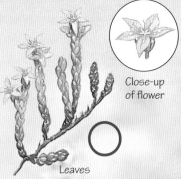

Close-up
of flower

Leaves

⬅ PURSLANE
A low, spreading plant
with red stems. The fleshy,
oval-shaped leaves are
in opposite pairs. A weed
of fields and waste places
May-Oct.

Close-up
of flower

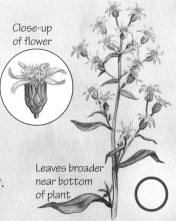

➡ GOLDEN ROD
Erect plant with flowers
on thin spikes. Leaves
are narrower and more
pointed near top of plant.
Woods, banks and cliffs.
40cm tall. July-Sept.

Leaves broader
near bottom
of plant

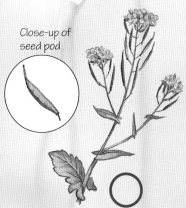
Close-up of seed pod

← RAPE

Common on roadsides, fields and motorways. Also grown as a crop. Dark blue-green leaves. Flowers grow in clusters and have four petals. Look for the long seed pods. Up to 100cm tall. May-July.

→ CYPRESS SPURGE

Erect plant with many pale, needle-like leaves. Spray of yellowish flowers. Roadsides and grassy places. Rare in Britain. 40cm tall. May-Aug.

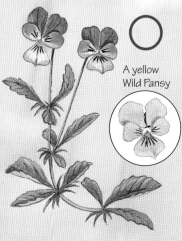
A yellow Wild Pansy

← WILD PANSY or HEARTSEASE

The flowers can be violet, yellow, or a mixture of both, or sometimes pink and white. Grassy places and cornfields. 15cm tall. April-Oct.

21

BLUE FLOWERS

◀ CORNFLOWER
Also called Bluebottle.
Erect plant with greyish,
downy leaves and a
blue flower head.
Cornfields and waste
places. 40cm tall.
July-Aug. Rare.

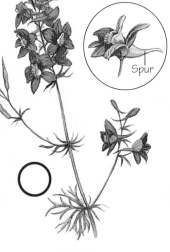

Seed pod

Spur

➤ LARKSPUR
Slender plant with
divided, feathery leaves.
The flowers have a long
spur. Cultivated land.
50cm tall. June-July.

Bud

◀ LESSER PERIWINKLE
Creeps along the
ground with long
runners, making leafy
carpets. Shiny, oval
leaves. Woods and
hedges. Flower stems up
to 15cm tall. Feb.-May.

Runner

Runner

For a link to a site about plants in different UK habitats, turn to page 59.

➡ VIPER'S BUGLOSS

Long, narrow leaves on rough, hairy stems. Erect or creeping. Pink buds become blue flowers. Waysides and sand dunes. 30cm tall. June-Sept.

Bud

Stamens

Sharp hairs on stem

Flowers have yellow centres

Rosette of leaves

⬅ COMMON FORGET-ME-NOT

The curled stems of this hairy plant slowly straighten when it flowers. Flowers turn from pink to blue. Open places. 20cm tall. April-Oct.

Close-up of flower

➡ COMMON SPEEDWELL

A hairy plant which forms large mats. Pinkish-blue flowers on erect spikes. Opposite, oval leaves. Grassy places and woods. 30cm tall. May-Aug.

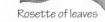

23

BLUE FLOWERS

Look for these flowers in damp places.

Flower is shaped like a monk's hood

◤ COMMON MONKSHOOD

Also called Wolfsbane. Upright plant with spike of flowers at end of stem. Notice hood on flowers and the deeply-divided leaves. Near streams and in damp woods. 70cm tall. June-Sept.

◥ BROOKLIME

Creeping plant with erect, reddish stems. Shiny, oval leaves in opposite pairs. Used to be eaten in salads. Wet places. 30cm tall. May-Sept.

Close-up of bugle-shaped flower

◀ BUGLE

Creeping plant with erect flower spikes. Glossy leaves in opposite pairs. Stem is square and hairy on two sides. Leaves and stem are purplish. Forms carpets in damp woods. 20cm tall. May-June.

➡ SEA HOLLY

A stiff, spiny plant with grey-blue leaves and round flower heads. Look for it on sandy and shingle beaches. 50cm tall. July-Aug.

Fruiting head

Flower

Flowers grow in whorls

⬅ MEADOW CLARY or MEADOW SAGE

Hairy stem with wrinkled leaves mostly at the base of the plant. Grassy places. 40cm tall. June-July.

➡ BLUEBELL

Also called Wild Hyacinth. Narrow, shiny leaves and clusters of nodding blue flowers. Forms thick carpets in woods. 30cm tall. April-May.

Close-up of fruit

PINK FLOWERS

Look for these flowers in woods or hedges.

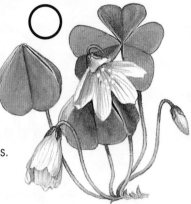

➡ WOOD SORREL
A creeping, woodland plant with slender stems and rounded leaves. The white flowers have purplish veins. Woods and hedges. 10cm tall. April-May.

◀ RED HELLEBORINE
Upright plant with pointed leaves and a fleshy stem. Rare plant, protected by law. Woods and shady places. Up to 40cm tall. May-June.

Ripe berry

➡ BLACKBERRY or BRAMBLE
Dense, woody plant that climbs up hedges. Sharp prickles on stems and under leaves. Berries are ripe and good to eat in autumn. June-Sept.

◀ BISTORT
Also called Snakeweed.
Forms patches. Leaves
are narrow. Flowers in
spikes. In meadows,
often near water.
40cm tall. June-Oct.

▶ GREATER BINDWEED
Look for the large, pink
or white funnel-shaped
flowers. Climbs walls and
hedges in waste places.
Leaves are shaped like
arrowheads. 300cm high.
July-Sept.

Bud

◀ DOG ROSE
Scrambling creeper,
up to 300cm tall,
with thorny stems.
Look for the red fruits,
called rose hips, in
autumn. Hedges and
woods. June-July.

Rose hip
(fruit)

27

PINK FLOWERS

➡ KNOTGRASS
A weed that spreads in a thick mat or grows erect. Waste ground, fields and seashores. Stems can be 100cm long. July-Oct.

Close-up of flower

◀ SOAPWORT
Erect plant with clusters of scented flowers. The broad, oval leaves were once used to make soap. Near rivers and streams. 40cm tall. Aug.-Oct.

Bud

Close-up of flower

➡ COMMON FUMITORY
Creeping plant with much-divided, feathery leaves. Tiny flowers are tube-shaped and tipped with purple. Cultivated land. 30cm tall. May-Oct.

For a link to a website about wild flower conservation, turn to page 59.

➡ SAND SPURREY
Spreading, mat-forming plant with sticky, hairy stems. Narrow, grey-green leaves end in a stiff point. Sandy places. 10cm tall. May-Sept.

Seed with hairy "parachute"

◀ ROSEBAY WILLOWHERB
Also called Fireweed. Tall, erect plant with spikes of pink flowers. Long, narrow leaves. Common on waste ground. 90cm tall. July-Sept.

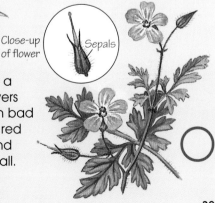

Close-up of flower
Sepals

➡ HERB ROBERT
Spreading plant with a strong smell. The flowers droop at night and in bad weather. Leaves are red in autumn. Woods and hedgebanks. 40cm tall. May-Sept.

29

PINK FLOWERS

Look for these flowers on heaths and moors.

Close-up of flower

☛ HEATHER or LING
Shrubby plant with small, narrow leaves. Grows on heaths and moors. Leafy spikes of pink or white flowers. 20cm tall. July-Sept.

➡ BELL HEATHER
Like Heather, but taller. Thin, needle-like leaves and clusters of bell-shaped, pink flowers. Dry heaths and moors. 30cm tall. July-Aug.

Close-up of flower

The berries are edible

⬅ BILBERRY
Small shrub with oval leaves. Drooping, bell-shaped, green-pink flowers. Heaths, moors and woods. 40cm tall. April-June.

Look for these flowers in
dry, grassy places.

➡ SORREL
Erect plant. Arrow-shaped
leaves have backward-
pointing lobes. Branched
spikes of flowers. Leaves
are eaten in salads.
Pastures. 20-100cm tall.

*Close-up
of flower
(above)
and fruit
(below)*

Lobe

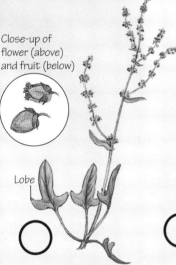

*Close-up of
flower (above)
and fruit (below)*

Lobe

⬅ SHEEP'S SORREL
Smaller than Sorrel.
The lobes on the
leaves point upwards.
Dry places and heaths.
30cm tall. May-Aug.

➡ COMMON CENTAURY
Erect plant with rosette of
leaves at base and opposite
leaves on stem. Flowers close
at night. Grassland, dunes
and woods. 50cm tall.
June-Oct.

*Opposite
pair of leaves*

PINK FLOWERS

➡ RAGGED ROBIN
Flowers have ragged, pink petals. Erect plant with a forked stem and narrow, pointed leaves. Damp meadows, marshes and woods. 30-70cm tall. May-June.

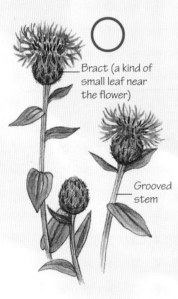

Bract (a kind of small leaf near the flower)

Grooved stem

◀ KNAPWEED or HARD-HEAD
Erect plant with brush-like, pink flowers growing from black bracts. Grassland and waysides. 40cm tall. June-Sept.

Whorl of leaves

➡ HEMP AGRIMONY
Tough, erect plant with downy stem. Grows in patches in damp places. Attracts butterflies. Up to 120cm tall. July-Sept.

◀ DEPTFORD PINK

The clusters of bright pink flowers close in the afternoon. Pointed, opposite leaves. Very rare in Britain. Sandy places. 40cm tall. July-Aug.

Close-up of flower

Fruit

➡ BLOOD-RED GERANIUM or BLOODY CRANESBILL

Bushy plant with erect or trailing stems. Deeply divided leaves are round and hairy. Hedgerows. 30cm tall. June-Aug.

Seed pod

◀ RED CAMPION

Erect plant with a hairy, sticky stem and pointed, oval leaves in opposite pairs. Woodland. 60cm tall. May-June.

33

PURPLE FLOWERS

◀ EARLY PURPLE ORCHID
Erect plant with dark spots on the leaves. Smells like cats. Look for the hood and spur on the flowers. Woods and copses. Up to 60cm tall. June-Aug.

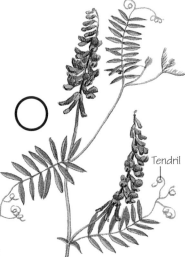

Tendril

➡ TUFTED VETCH
Scrambling plant with clinging tendrils. Climbs up hedgerows. Look for the brown seed pods in late summer. Flowers 1cm across. June-Sept.

Policeman's Helmet

Touch-me-not Balsam

◀ POLICEMAN'S HELMET
Also called Jumping Jack. Flowers look like open mouths. Ripe seed pods explode, scattering seeds when touched. Streams. Up to 200cm tall. July-Oct.

Policeman's Helmet is closely related to Touch-me-not Balsam

Look for these flowers in woods or hedgerows.

➡ FOXGLOVE

Erect plant with tall spike of tube-shaped flowers, drooping on one side of the stem. Large, oval leaves. Open woods. Up to 150cm tall. June-Sept.

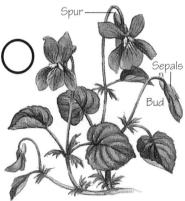

➡ BATS-IN-THE-BELFRY

Erect, hairy plant with large, toothed leaves. Flowers on leafy spikes point upwards. Hedges, woods and shady places. 60cm tall. July-Sept.

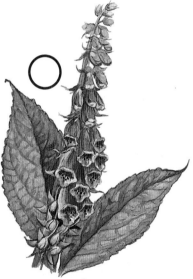

⬅ COMMON DOG VIOLET

Creeping plant with rosettes of heart-shaped leaves. Look for the pointed sepals and short spur on the flower. Woods. 10cm tall. April-June.

35

For a link to a site about wild flowers near your home, turn to page 59.

PURPLE FLOWERS

Look in fields and other grassy places for these flowers.

➡ PASQUE FLOWER
Very rare in the wild, but grows in gardens. Hairy, feathery leaves. Purple or white flowers have yellow anthers. Dry, grassy places. 10cm tall. April-May.

Devil's Bit Scabious

Field Scabious

Field Scabious is a similar species

⬅ DEVIL'S BIT SCABIOUS
Erect plant with narrow, pointed leaves. Flowers are pale to dark purple. Round flower heads. Wet, grassy places. 15-30cm tall. June-Oct.

Lobed leaves

Entire leaves

➡ FRITILLARY or SNAKE'S HEAD
Drooping flowers are chequered with light and dark purple. Varies from white to dark purple. Damp meadows. 10cm tall. May.

You may see these
flowers on old walls.

➡ IVY-LEAVED TOADFLAX
Weak, slender stalks trail
on old walls. Look for the
yellow lips on the mauve
flowers. Flowers 1cm across.
Shiny, ivy-shaped leaves.
May-Sept.

*The stalk, with
flowers, does
not appear
very often –
usually you
will see only
the rosette*

⬅ HOUSELEEK
A rosette plant with thick,
fleshy leaves. Dull red, spiky
petals. Does not flower
every year. Old walls
and roofs. 30-60cm tall.
June-July.

Rosette of leaves

➡ SNAPDRAGON
Erect plant with spike of
flowers. Long, narrow
leaves. Pouch-like flowers
are yellow inside. Old
walls, rocks and gardens.
40cm tall. June-Sept.

Fruit

37

RED FLOWERS

Look for these flowers on cultivated land.

Flowers may also be blue

➡ SCARLET PIMPERNEL
Grows along the ground.
Flowers close in bad
weather. Black dots
under the pointed,
oval leaves.
Cultivated land.
15cm tall.
June-Aug.

➡ POPPY
Erect plant with stiff hairs
on stem. Soft, red flowers
have dark centres. Round
seed pod. Cornfields and
waste ground. Up to
60cm tall. June-Aug.

Seed pod

Bud

Seed pod

⬅ LONG-HEADED POPPY
Like Poppy, but flowers are
paler and do not have dark
centres. Pod is long and
narrow. Cornfields and
waste ground. Up to 45cm
tall. June-Aug.

← PHEASANT'S EYE

Rare cornfield weed with finely divided, feathery leaves. The red flowers have black centres. 20cm tall. May-Sept.

Summer Pheasant's Eye (not in Britain) is a similar species

→ SWEET WILLIAM

Tough, narrow leaves and flat flower cluster. Mountain pastures and cultivated land in Europe. Gardens only in Britain. 60cm tall. May-June.

Close-up of flower

← WOOD WOUNDWORT

The leaves were once used to dress wounds. Spikes of dark red and white flowers in whorls. Smells strongly. Woods. 40cm tall. June-Aug.

WHITE AND GREEN FLOWERS

These flowers can be
found in woodlands
quite early in the year.

Split petals

➡ GREATER STITCHWORT
Look in woods and
hedgerows for this slender,
creeping plant. Grass-like
leaves in opposite pairs.
15-60cm tall. April-June.

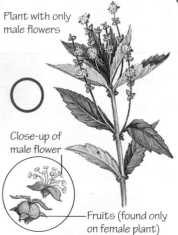

Plant with only
male flowers

Close-up of
male flower

Fruits (found only
on female plant)

◀ DOG'S MERCURY
Downy plant with
opposite, toothed
leaves. Strong-smelling.
Male flowers grow on
separate plants from
female flowers. Found
in patches in woodlands.
15-20cm tall. Feb.-April.

Berry

➡ LILY-OF-THE-VALLEY
Grows in dry woods.
Broad, dark green leaves
and sweet-smelling flowers.
Red berries in summer.
Also a garden plant.
20cm tall. May-June.

For a link to a virtual tour of Kew Gardens, turn to page 59.

➡ RAMSONS or WOOD GARLIC

Smells of garlic.
Broad, bright green
leaves grow from a bulb.
Forms carpets in damp
woods, often with
Bluebells. 10-25cm tall.
April-June.

Notice the
long veins that
run from one
end of the leaf
to the other

The large sepals
look like petals

⬅ WOOD ANEMONE

Also called Granny's
Nightcap. Forms
carpets in woods.
The flowers have
pink-streaked sepals.
15cm tall. March-June.

➡ SNOWDROP

Welcomed as the first
flower of the new year.
Dark green, narrow
leaves. Nodding
white flowers. Woods.
20cm tall. Jan.-March.

41

WHITE AND GREEN FLOWERS

Look for these flowers in hedges or woods.

— Seed pod

◣ JACK-BY-THE-HEDGE or GARLIC MUSTARD
Erect plant with heart-shaped, toothed leaves. Smells of garlic. Common in hedges. Up to 120cm tall. April-June.

➡ WILD STRAWBERRY
Small plant with long, arching runners and oval, toothed leaves in threes. Sweet, red fruits, covered with seeds. Woods and scrubland. April-July.

Fruits are smaller than garden strawberries

— Tendril

◀ WILD PEA
Very rare, scrambling plant with grey-green leaves. The seeds, or peas, are inside the pods. Climbs on thickets and hedges. Up to 250cm high. June-Aug.

Pod

Look for these flowers in
hedges and waysides.

➡ WHITE BRYONY
Climbs up hedges with
spiral tendrils. The red
berries appear in August
and are poisonous. Large
underground stems, called
tubers. Up to 400cm tall. June.

Close-up of
female flower

Tendril

Berries

⬅ COW PARSLEY
Also called Lady's Lace.
Look for the ribbed stem,
feathery leaves and white
flower clusters. Hedge
banks and ditches. Up
to 100cm tall. May-June.

Close-up
of flower

Fruit

➡ HEDGE PARSLEY
Like Cow Parsley, but with
a stiff, hairy stem. Look for
the prickly, purple fruits.
Cornfields and roadsides.
60cm tall. April-May

Close-up
of flower

Fruit

43

WHITE AND GREEN FLOWER.

These flowers can be found in or near fresh water, such as streams and ponds.

➡ MEADOWSWEET
Clusters of sweet-smelling flowers. Grows in marshes, water meadows and also near ditches at the side of the road. Up to 80cm tall. May-Sept.

Undersides of leaves are silvery-grey

◀ TRIANGULAR-STALKED GARLIC or THREE-CORNERED LEEK
Smells of garlic. Drooping flowers. In damp hedges and waste places. 40cm tall. June-July.

The flower stem is three-sided

➡ FLOATING WATER PLANTAIN
Water plant with oval leaves and white flowers on the water surface. Look for it in canals and still water. Flowers 1-1.5cm across. May-Aug.

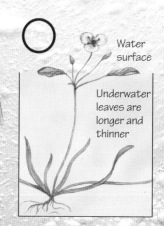
Water surface

Underwater leaves are longer and thinner

➡ WATER CROWFOOT

Water plant whose roots are anchored in the mud at the bottom of ponds and streams. Flowers (1-2cm across) cover the water surface. May-June.

These leaves are on the water surface

Fine, underwater leaves

◀ WATER SOLDIER

Under water except when it flowers. Long, saw-like leaves then show above the surface. Flowers 3-4cm across. Ponds, canals, ditches. June-Aug.

Bud

➡ FROGBIT

Rises to the surface in spring, and spreads with long runners. Shiny, round leaves grow in tufts. Flowers 2cm across. Canals and ponds. July-Aug.

Runner

WHITE AND GREEN FLOWERS

Look for these flowers in fields and other grassy places.

Clusters of small flowers

Close-up of single flower

➡ WILD CARROT
Dense clusters of white flowers with a purple flower in the centre. Erect, hairy stem with feathery leaves. Grassy places, often near coast. 60cm tall. July-Aug.

Bracts

Fruit

Clusters of fruits

Close-up of single flower

Fruit

⬅ HOGWEED or KECK
Very stout, hairy plant with huge leaves on long stalks. Flowers are in clusters. Grassy places and open woods. Up to 100cm tall. June-Sept.

➡ CORKY-FRUITED WATER DROPWORT
Erect plant with large, much-divided, feathery leaves. Clusters of flowers. Meadows. 60cm tall. June-Aug.

Single flower

Fruit

White petals are sometimes tinged with pink

← DAISY
Small plant with rosette of leaves at base. Flowers close at night and in bad weather. Very common on garden lawns. 10cm tall. Jan.-Oct.

→ WHITE or DUTCH CLOVER
Creeping plant, often grown for animal feed. Look for the white band on the three-lobed leaves. Attracts bees. 10-25cm tall. April-Aug.

White band

Look for the divided petals

Runner

← FIELD MOUSE-EAR CHICKWEED
Creeping plant with erect stems. Narrow, downy leaves. Grassy places. 10cm tall. April-Aug.

WHITE AND GREEN FLOWERS

Look for these flowers on cultivated land, waste land and waysides.

Close-up of flower

➤ COMMON ORACHE

An erect weed with a stiff stem and toothed leaves, both dusty grey. Cultivated land or waste places. Up to 90cm tall. Aug.-Sept.

Close-up of flower

➤ PIGWEED or COMMON AMARANTH

Erect, hairy plant with large, oval leaves. Large spikes of green, tufty flowers. Look for it on cultivated land. 50cm tall. July-Sept.

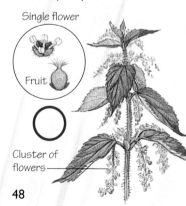

Single flower

Fruit

◄ NETTLE

The toothed leaves are covered with stinging hairs. Dangling green-brown flowers. Used to make beer and tea. Common. Up to 100cm tall. June-Aug.

Cluster of flowers

➡ GOOD KING HENRY

An erect plant with arrow-shaped leaves and spikes of tiny, green flowers. Farmyards and roadsides. 30-50cm tall. May-July.

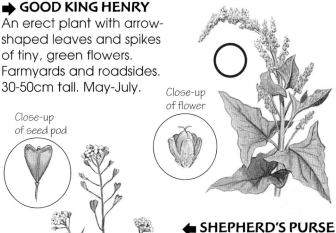

Close-up of flower

Close-up of seed pod

⬅ SHEPHERD'S PURSE

Very common plant. The white flowers and heart-shaped seed pods can be seen all year round. Waysides and waste places. Up to 40cm tall.

Rosette of leaves

➡ WHITE DEAD-NETTLE

Looks like Nettle, but the hairs do not sting. Flowers in whorls on the stem. Hedgerows and waste places. Up to 60cm tall. May-Dec.

Note the "hoods" on the flowers

49

WHITE AND GREEN FLOWERS

➡ BLADDER CAMPION
Oval leaves in opposite
pairs. The sepals are
joined together, forming
a bladder. Grassy places
and hedgerows. 30cm
tall. June-Sept.

Calyx is smaller
than that of
Bladder Campion

When flowering
is over, fruit
grows inside
sepals (calyx)

⬅ WHITE CAMPION
The erect stems and
the sepals are sticky
and hairy. The white
petals are divided.
Look in hedgerows.
Up to 100cm tall.
May-June.

➡ CORN SPURREY
Spindly plant with
jointed, sticky stems.
Narrow leaves in whorls
around the stem. Weed
of cornfields. 30cm tall.
April-July.

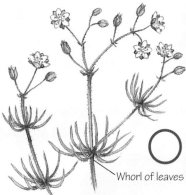

Whorl of leaves

50

For a link to a website with flowery e-cards to send, turn to page 59.

◄ CHICKWEED
Mat-forming plant
with stems that can
grow up to 40cm tall.
You can see the small
flowers all year round.
Common weed in
fields and gardens.

➧ BLACK NIGHTSHADE
Shrubby weed of
cultivated ground. Shiny,
oval leaves. Petals fold
back to show yellow
anthers. The berries are
poisonous. 20cm tall.
July-Sept.

Anthers

Berries

Whorl
of leaves

Fruit

◄ GOOSEGRASS or COMMON CLEAVERS
Scrambling plant. The
prickly stems stick to
clothes and animal fur.
Hedges. 60cm tall.
June-Sept.

WHITE AND GREEN FLOWERS

Look for these flowers in grassy places, on waste or cultivated ground.

Anthers

▲ RIBWORT PLANTAIN or COCKS AND HENS

Tough plant with narrow, ribbed leaves. Green-brown spikes of flowers have white anthers. Common. 20cm tall. April-Aug.

Anthers are mauve at first, changing to yellow

Anthers

➡ GREATER PLANTAIN or RATSTAIL

Broad-ribbed leaves in a rosette close to the ground. All kinds of cultivated land. 15cm tall. May-Sept.

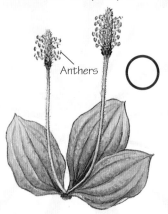

Anthers

◀ HOARY PLANTAIN

Rosette plant with oval, ribbed leaves. Fine hairs on stem. White flowers have purple anthers. Common in grassy places. 7-15cm tall. May-Aug.

Look for these flowers on grassy or waste ground.

← YARROW
Common plant with rough stem and feathery leaves. Flat-topped clusters of flowers. Smells sweet. Was once used to heal wounds. 40cm tall. June-Aug.

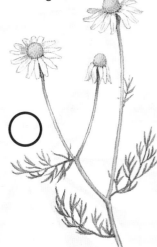

→ WILD CHAMOMILE or SCENTED MAYWEED
Erect plant with finely divided leaves. The petals fold back. Waste places everywhere. 15-40cm tall. June-July.

← OX-EYE DAISY or MARGUERITE
Erect plant with rosette of toothed leaves and large, daisy-like flowers. Roadsides and grassy places. Up to 60cm tall. June-Aug.

WHITE AND GREEN FLOWERS

➡ STARRY SAXIFRAGE
A rosette plant with shiny, fleshy, toothed leaves. Mountain rocks. 20cm tall. June-Aug.

➡ MEADOW SAXIFRAGE
Downy, lobed leaves. Up to 40cm tall. Grassy places.

Meadow Saxifrage

Starry Saxifrage

Rosette of leaves

Seed pods

⬅ ALPINE ROCK CRESS
Short, mat-forming plant with rosette of greyish-green leaves. Dense clusters of white flowers. Rocks on hills and mountains. April-June.

Close-up of flower

➡ PELLITORY-OF-THE-WALL
Plant with red stems and soft hairs. Tiny, stalkless green flowers. Cracks in rocks and walls, and hedgebanks. Up to 100cm tall. June-Oct.

PROTECTING WILD FLOWERS

Be careful not to tread on young plants or to break their stems.

Many wild plants that were once common are now rare, because people have picked and dug up so many. It is now against the law to dig up any wild plant by the roots, or to pick certain rare plants such as the Red Helleborine. If you pick wild flowers, they will die. Leave them for others to enjoy. It is much better to draw or photograph flowers, so that you and other people can see them again.

Red Helleborine

The Pasque flower is rare in the wild

If you think you have found a rare plant, let your local nature conservation club know about it as soon as you can, so they can help protect it. You can get their address from your local library or look on the Web. There is a list of useful websites on page 59.

FLOWER NOTEBOOK

You could record everything you discover about wild flowers in a notebook. Draw one plant on each page. Note its height, and when and where you found it. Note down anything else you notice, like butterflies and insects feeding or laying eggs on it. Try choosing a particular area to study.

Find a place where plants grow undisturbed, like a churchyard or a grassy verge. Mark out a square metre of ground with sticks and string. Identify and count the flowers you see. Try to find out why these plants grow in the same area. Keep a record of how they change in different seasons.

PHOTOGRAPHING FLOWERS

Photographs make a good record of the flowers you spot. If you take photographs while spotting, put them in your flower notebook along with your drawings and notes about flowers.

If you are photographing a flower, try to keep the sun behind you. Make sure your shadow doesn't fall on the flower, though. Try lying on the ground and photographing the flower from below, so it is outlined clearly against the sky. To prevent a flower from being lost among grass and leaves, try propping a piece of card behind it to make a plain background.

Tall plants with large flowers usually look best in photographs

Include the stems and seed pods in your picture

USEFUL WORDS

This page explains some of the specialist words used in this book. Words that appear in *italic* text are defined separately.

anther - the top part of the *stamen*. It produces pollen.

bract - a leaf-like structure at the base of a flower or stalk.

bulb - a mass of thick, fleshy leaves which store food for a plant under the ground.

calyx - a name for all the *sepals* together.

carpel - the female part of the flower. It consists of the *stigma*, *style* and *ovary*.

corolla - all the *petals*.

filament - the stalk of the *stamen*. It supports the *anther*.

flowerhead - a cluster of small flowers. It often looks like a single flower.

nectar - a sweet liquid produced by some plants to attract insects.

ovary - the part of the flower where seeds are produced.

petal - a segment of the *corolla*, usually brightly coloured.

pollination - when pollen reaches the *stigma*.

runner - a stem that grows along the ground.

sepals - leaf or petal-like growths which protect the flower bud and support the flower once it opens.

spur - a tube formed by the petals of some flowers. It often contains *nectar*.

stamens - the male parts of the flower. Each stamen is made up of an *anther* and a *filament*.

stigma - the top part of the *carpel*. It receives the pollen when the flower is pollinated.

style - part of the *carpel*. It joins the *stigma* to the *ovary*.

tendril - a thin stem or leaf that helps a plant to climb.

tuber - a large, underground stem.

weed - a plant that grows on waste or cultivated land, often getting in the way of other plants.

INTERNET LINKS

If you have access to the Internet, you can visit these websites to find out more about wild flowers. For links to these sites, go to the Usborne Quicklinks Website at **www.usborne-quicklinks.com** and enter the keywords "spotters wild flowers".

Internet safety

When using the Internet, please follow the **Internet safety guidelines** shown on the Usborne Quicklinks Website.

WEBSITE 1 An online guide to help you identify wild flowers.

WEBSITE 2 Another online guide to help you identify wild flowers.

WEBSITE 3 Photos and information about the wild flowers found in Britain.

WEBSITE 4 A national UK postcode database allowing you to find out about wild flowers near your home.

WEBSITE 5 Discover the plant life in different habitats around the UK.

WEBSITE 6 A colourful introduction to plant biology, with lots of pictures.

WEBSITE 7 Lots of information about wild plant conservation and the effects of climate change, plus interactive wild flowers.

WEBSITE 8 Take a virtual tour of Kew Gardens, the UK's leading plant conservation centre.

WEBSITE 9 Send a flowery e-card.

SCORECARD

The flowers in this scorecard are arranged in alphabetical order. When you spot a species, fill in the date next to its score. Rare species score more than common ones.

After a day's spotting, add up all the points you have scored on a sheet of paper and keep a note of them. See if you can score more points another day.

Species (Name of flower)	Score	Date spotted	Species (Name of flower)	Score	Date spotted
Alpine Rock Cress	20		Common Dog Violet	10	
Alternate-leaved Golden Saxifrage	15		Common Forget-me-not	10	
Barberry	15		Common Fumitory	10	
Bats-in-the-belfry	15		Common Meadow Rue	15	
Bell Heather	15		Common Monkshood	20	
Bilberry	10		Common Orache	5	
Bird's Foot Trefoil	10		Common Speedwell	10	
Bistort	10		Common St. John's Wort	10	
Black Nightshade	10		Corky-fruited Water Dropwart	25	
Blackberry	5		Corn Spurrey	10	
Bladder Campion	5		Cornflower	25	
Blood-red Geranium	10		Cow Parsley	5	
Bluebell	10		Cowslip	10	
Brooklime	10		Creeping Buttercup	5	
Bugle	10		Creeping Cinquefoil	5	
Chickweed	5		Creeping Jenny	15	
Common Centaury	10		Cypress Spurge	15	

Species (Name of flower)	Score	Date spotted	Species (Name of flower)	Score	Date spotted
Daisy	5		Hoary Plantain	5	
Dandelion	5		Hogweed	10	
Deptford Pink	25		Houseleek	15	
Devil's Bit Scabious	10		Ivy-leaved Toadflax	5	
Dog Rose	15		Jack-by-the-hedge	5	
Dog's Mercury	10		Knapweed	10	
Early Purple Orchid	15		Knotgrass	5	
Field Scabious	10		Larkspur	15	
Field Mouse-ear Chickweed	15		Lesser Celandine	5	
Floating Water Plantain	15		Lesser Periwinkle	15	
Foxglove	10		Lily-of-the-valley	15	
Fritillary	20		Long-headed Poppy	5	
Frogbit	15		Meadow Clary	20	
Furze	10		Meadow Saxifrage	20	
Golden Rod	10		Meadowsweet	10	
Good King Henry	5		Nettle	10	
Goosegrass	5		Ox-eye Daisy	10	
Greater Bindweed	10		Pasque Flower	25	
Greater Plantain	5		Pellitory-of-the-wall	15	
Greater Stitchwort	5		Pheasant's Eye	25	
Heather	5		Pigweed	10	
Hedge Parsley	15		Policeman's Helmet	15	
Hemp Agrimony	10		Poppy	10	
Herb Bennet	10		Primrose	10	
Herb Robert	10		Purslane	15	

Species (Name of flower)	Score	Date spotted	Species (Name of flower)	Score	Date spotted
Ragged Robin	15		Triangular-stalked Garlic	20	
Ramsons	15		Tufted Vetch	10	
Rape	5		Viper's Bugloss	10	
Red Campion	10		Water Crowfoot	10	
Red Helleborine	25		Water Soldier	25	
Ribwort Plantain	5		White Bryony	15	
Rosebay Willowherb	5		White Campion	10	
Sand Spurrey	10		White Clover	5	
Scarlet Pimpernel	10		White Dead-Nettle	5	
Sea Holly	15		Wild Carrot	10	
Sheep's Sorrel	15		Wild Chamomile	15	
Shepherd's Purse	5		Wild Pansy	10	
Silverweed	10		Wild Pea	20	
Snapdragon	5		Wild Strawberry	15	
Snowdrop	15		Woad	20	
Soapwort	20		Wood Anemone	10	
Sorrel	5		Wood Groundsel	15	
Starry Saxifrage	15		Wood Sorrel	5	
Stonecrop	10		Wood Woundwort	10	
Summer Pheasant's Eye	25		Yarrow	5	
Sweet William	20		Yellow Archangel	10	
Touch-me-not Balsam	25		Yellow Pimpernel	10	

INDEX

Agrimony, Hemp, 32
Amaranth, Common,
    see Pigweed
Anemone, Wood, 41
Archangel, Yellow, 17
Avens, Wood,
    see Herb Bennet

Bacon and Eggs,
    see Trefoil, Bird's Foot
Balsam, Touch-me-not, 34
Barberry, 16
Bats-in-the-belfry, 35
Bilberry, 30
Bindweed, Greater, 27
Bistort, 27
Blackberry, 11, 26
Bluebell, 25
Bluebottle, *see* Cornflower
Bramble, *see* Blackberry
Brooklime, 24
Bryony, White, 43
Bugle, 24
Bugloss, Viper's, 23
Buttercup, 8, 10
    Creeping, 9, 14

Campion,
    Bladder, 50
    Red, 33
    White, 50
Carrot, Wild, 46
Celandine, Lesser, 14
Centaury, Common, 31
Chamomile, Wild, 53
Chickweed, 51
    Field Mouse-ear, 47
Cinquefoil, Creeping, 18
Clary, Meadow, 10, 25
Cleavers, Common,
    see Goosegrass
Clover, White or Dutch, 47
Cocks and Hens,
    see Plantain, Ribwort
Cornflower, 22
Cowslip, 15
Cranesbill, Bloody,
    see Geranium, Blood-red
Creeping Jenny, 15
Cress, Alpine Rock, 54

Daisy, 8, 47
    Ox-eye, 53
Dandelion, 19
Dead-Nettle, White, 49
Dropwort,
    Corky-fruited Water, 46

Fireweed,
    see Willowherb, Rosebay
Forget-me-not, Common, 23
Foxglove, 8, 35
Fritillary, 36
Frogbit, 45
Fumitory, Common, 28
Furze, 18

Garlic, Triangular-stalked, 44
    Wood, *see* Ramsons
Geranium, Blood-red, 33
Golden Rod, 20
Good King Henry, 49
Goosegrass, 51
Gorse, *see* Furze
Granny's Nightcap,
    see Anemone, Wood
Groundsel, Wood, 17

Hard-head, *see* Knapweed
Heartsease, *see* Pansy, Wild
Heather, 30
    Bell, 30
Helleborine, Red, 26, 55
Herb Bennet, 16
Herb Robert, 29
Hogweed, 46
Holly, Sea, 25
Houseleek, 37
Hyacinth, Wild, *see* Bluebell

Jack-by-the-hedge, 42
Jumping Jack,
    see Policeman's Helmet

Keck, *see* Hogweed
Knapweed, 32
Knotgrass, 28

Lady's Lace, *see* Parsley, Cow
Larkspur, 22
Leek, Three-cornered,
    see Garlic, Triangular-stalked
Lily-of-the-valley, 40
Ling, *see* Heather

Marguerite,
    see Daisy, Ox-eye
Mayweed, Scented,
    see Chamomile, Wild
Meadow Rue, Common, 15
Meadowsweet, 44
Mercury, Dog's, 40
Monkshood, Common, 24
Mustard, Garlic,
    see Jack-by-the-hedge

Nettle, 48
Nightshade, Black, 51

Orache, Common, 48
Orchid, Common Spotted, 8
Orchid, Early Purple, 9, 34

Pansy, Wild, 21
Parsley,
    Cow, 43
    Hedge, 43
Pasque Flower, 36, 55
Pea, Wild, 42
Pellitory-of-the-wall, 54
Periwinkle, Lesser, 22
Pheasant's Eye, 39
    Summer, 39
Pigweed, 48
Pimpernel,
    Scarlet, 5, 38
    Yellow, 16
Pink, Deptford, 33
Plantain,
    Floating Water, 44
    Greater, 52
    Hoary, 52
    Ribwort, 52
Policeman's Helmet, 34
Poppy, 11, 38
    Long-headed, 38
Primrose, 17
Purslane, 20

Ragged Robin, 32
Ramsons, 41
Rape, 21
Ratstail,
    see Plantain, Greater
Rose, Dog, 11, 27

Sage, Meadow,
    see Clary, Meadow

St John's Wort, Common, 19
Saxifrage,
    Alternate-leaved Golden, 14
    Meadow, 54
    Starry, 54
Scabious,
    Devil's Bit, 36
    Field, 36
Shepherd's Purse, 49
Silverweed, 18
Snake's Head,
    see Fritillary
Snakeweed,
    see Bistort
Snapdragon, 37
Snowdrop, 41
Soapwort, 28
Sorrel, 31
    Sheep's, 31
    Wood, 26
Speedwell, Common, 23
Spurge, Cypress, 21
Spurrey,
    Corn, 50
    Sand, 29
Stitchwort, Greater, 40
Stonecrop, 9, 20
Strawberry, Wild, 42
Sweet William, 39

Toadflax, 8
    Ivy-leaved, 37
Trefoil, Bird's Foot, 18

Vetch, Tufted, 34
Violet, Common Dog, 35

Wallpepper,
    see Stonecrop
Water Crowfoot, 45
Water Soldier, 45
Weasel-snout,
    see Archangel, Yellow
Whin, see Furze
Willowherb, Rosebay, 4, 29
Woad, 19
Wolfsbane,
    see Monkshood, Common
Woundwort, Wood, 39

Yarrow, 53